MY FIRST LITTLE HOUSE BOOKS

A LIT OUSE B AY

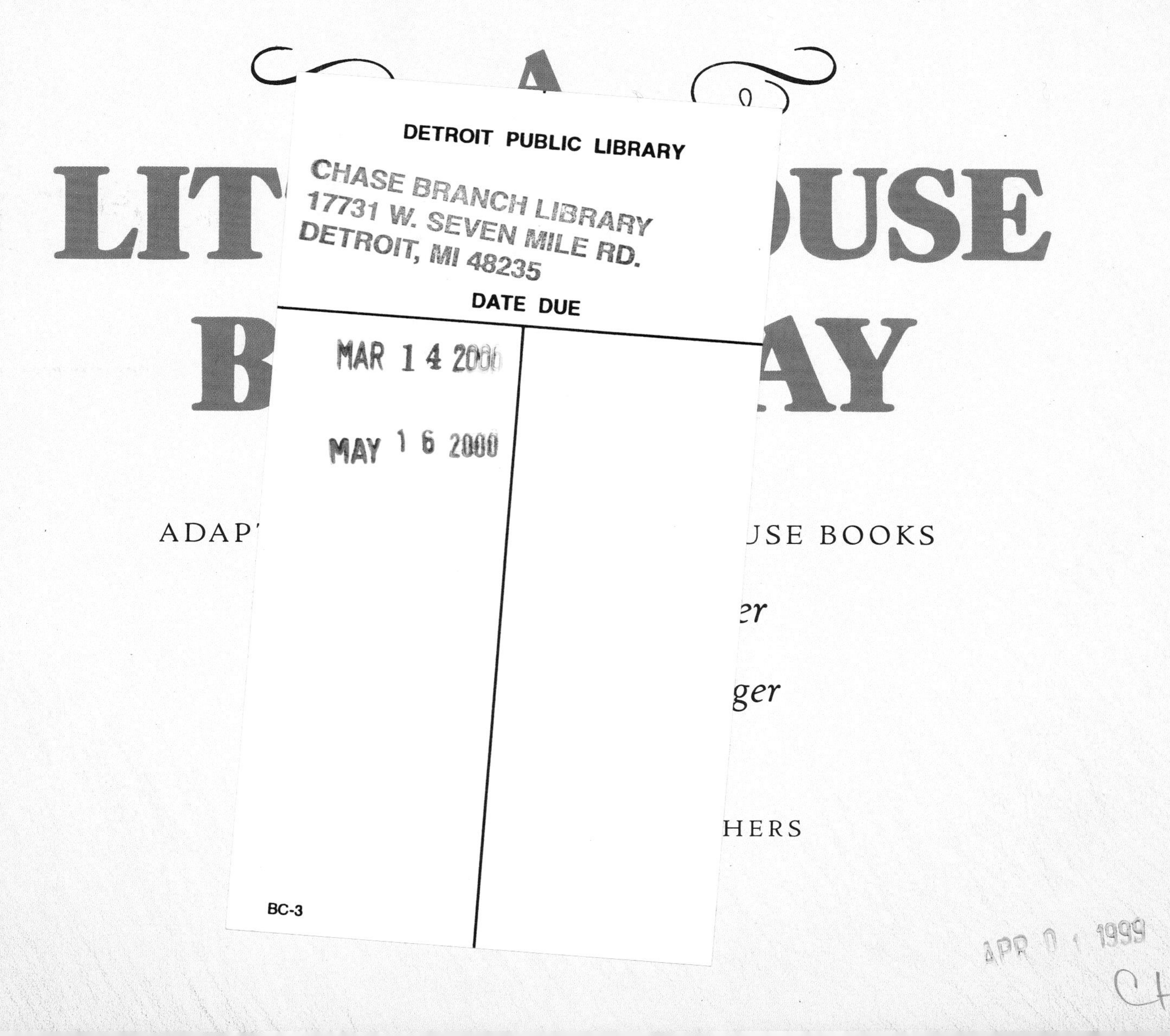

ADAP USE BOOKS

er

ger

HERS

For my mother,
Minnie Bush Ettlinger

—D. E.

A Little House Birthday Text adapted from Little House in the Big Woods *Text copyright 1932, copyright renewed 1959, Roger Lea MacBride. Illustrations copyright © 1997 by Renée Graef Printed in the U.S.A. All rights reserved. http://www.harperchildrens.com Library of Congress Cataloging-in-Publication Data A Little house birthday / adapted from The Little house books by Laura Ingalls Wilder ; illustrated by Doris Ettlinger. p. cm. — (My first Little house books) Text adapted from Little House in the Big Woods. Summary: After a long and somber Sunday, a little pioneer girl celebrates her fifth birthday in the Big Woods of Wisconsin. ISBN 0-06-025928-0. ISBN 0-06-025929-9 (lib. bdg.) — ISBN 0-06-443494-X (pbk.) [1. Wilder, Laura Ingalls, 1867–1957—Juvenile fiction. 2. Birthdays—Fiction. 3. Frontier and pioneer life—Fiction. 4. Family life—Fiction.] I. Wilder, Laura Ingalls, 1867–1957. Little house in the Big Woods. II. Ettlinger, Doris, ill. III. Series. PZ7.L7345 1997 96-41512 [E]—dc20 CIP AC ❖ HarperCollins®, ®, and Little House® are trademarks of HarperCollins Publishers Inc.*

Illustrations for the My First Little House Books are
inspired by the work of Garth Williams with his
permission, which we gratefully acknowledge.

Once upon a time, a little girl named Laura lived in the Big Woods of Wisconsin in a little house made of logs.

Laura lived in the little house with her Pa, her Ma, her big sister Mary, her little sister Carrie, and their good old bulldog Jack.

The winter seemed long, and Laura and Mary began to be tired of staying always in the house. Especially on Sundays, the time went so slowly.

Every Saturday night Pa filled the washtub with fresh snow and put the washtub on the cookstove. Soon the snow melted to water, and it was time for Laura and Mary to take their baths. Laura took her bath first, because she was littler than Mary. Then Mary had her bath, and then Ma had her bath, and then Pa had his.

Now they were all clean for Sunday, and on Sunday mornings Laura and Mary dressed in their best clothes with fresh ribbons in their hair. On Sundays they could not run or shout or be noisy. They must sit quietly and listen while Ma read stories to them. They might look at pictures, and they might hold their rag dolls nicely and talk to them. But there was nothing else they could do.

One Sunday Laura could not bear it any longer, and she began to play with Jack and run and shout. Pa told her to sit in her chair and be quiet, and Laura began to cry. So Pa took her on his knee and cuddled her and told her a story.

Soon that long Sunday was almost over, and Laura lay in her trundle bed with Mary listening to Pa sing Sunday hymns with the fiddle. The next sound she heard was Ma by the stove making breakfast. It was Monday, and Sunday would not come again for a whole week.

That morning when Pa came in to breakfast, he caught Laura and explained that today was her birthday! Laura was five years old.

Pa gave Laura a little wooden man he had whittled out of a stick, to be company for her rag doll, Charlotte. Ma gave her five little cakes, one for each year.

Mary gave her a new dress for Charlotte. Mary had made the dress herself, when Laura thought she was sewing on her patchwork quilt.

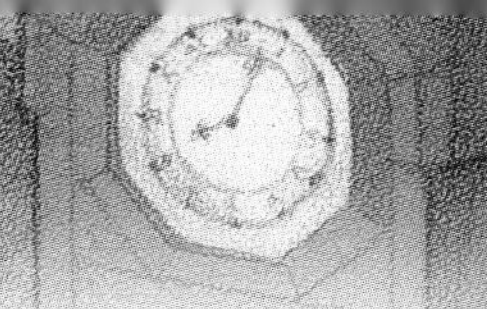

That night, for a special treat, Pa played "Pop Goes the Weasel" on his fiddle for Laura. "Now watch," he said. "Watch, and maybe you can see the weasel pop out this time."

Then he sang:

"All around the mulberry bush,
The monkey chased the weasel,
The monkey thought t'was all in fun,
Pop! goes the weasel.
A penny for a spool of thread,
A penny for a needle,
That's the way the money goes,
Pop! goes the weasel."

But Laura and Mary hadn't seen Pa's finger make the string pop. "Oh please, please do it again!" they begged him. Pa's blue eyes laughed, and the fiddle went on while he sang. But he was so quick, they could never catch him.

So they went laughing to bed and lay listening to Pa and the fiddle singing. It had been a happy birthday in the little house in the Big Woods.